For Joshua,
who first asked the question – F.S.

For Ruth, Johnny and Anna.
With all my love – B.C.

Hodder Children's Books

First published in Great Britain in 2013 by Orion Children's Books as *Do You Speak English, Moon?*
This edition published in 2019 by Hodder and Stoughton.

Text copyright © Francesca Simon, 2013
Illustrations copyright © Ben Cort, 2013, 2019

A CIP catalogue record for this book is available from the British Library.

ISBN 978 1 444 951 264

1 3 5 7 9 10 8 6 4 2

Printed and bound in China.

Hodder Children's Books
An imprint of Hachette Children's Group
Part of Hodder and Stoughton
Carmelite House
50 Victoria Embankment
London, EC4Y 0DZ

An Hachette UK Company
www.hachette.co.uk

www.hachettechildrens.co.uk

Hello Moon

FRANCESCA SIMON
BEN CORT

Hodder
Children's
Books

"Hello Moon. Can we talk?
I get lonely down
here sometimes.

What I want to know is...

...do you have a bouncy bed?

You don't?

Oh, that's sad.

I like bouncing on my bed.

Do you go to the park, Moon?
I can go down the
twisty, turny slide.

Do you like chocolate ice cream?
That is my very best food.

Do you pretend you're a crocodile?
Do you play pirates?

So do I!
What else do you do?

Ahhh. I like watching too.

Can you see everything, Moon?

Can you see the city?

Can you see the sea?

Can you see under the sea?

Can you see the highest, highest mountain?

Can you see
the whole wide world?
Oh show me, show me!

Do you have lots of friends, Moon?
A billion, trillion, gazillion?

But they're all so far away.

Can you tell me some of their names?

Leo.
That's a nice name.

Milky Way. I like that one too.

Pegasus. Pluto. Polaris. Little Bear.

Little Bear?

Oh, shh. She's asleep.
I'm supposed to be asleep too.

But sometimes
it's hard to get
to sleep.

Do you get lonely up there, Moon?

Don't be lonely.

I'm here.
Any time you want to talk.

Goodnight, Moon. Goodnight."

This book belongs to:

· ·